THE WOMPANANNY WITCHES MAKE ONE MEAN PIZZA

JENNIE PALMER

Abrams Books for Young Readers · New York

Anita and Winnifred Wompananny were kitchen witches.
They whipped up ravioli, cakes, and cannoli with glee.

But their passion was pizza.
And the pies they crafted were
delightfully delicious.

The two lived on a busy block, but they rarely ventured outside. Witches are wary of children, and the neighborhood kids seemed especially wild.

Beware of Cat!

Then one day,
the witches' doorbell buzzed.

HOT TOPPINGS! IT'S THREE CHILDREN!

Both witches hit the floor.
They held their breath until the children had gone.

The children had rattled the witches. So Anita and Winnifred needed to blow off some steam! Back in their kitchen, the two pounded their fearful, freaked-out feelings into fresh dough.

Then they slid the new pizza into the oven,
finally feeling sweet as sauce.

But they had baked all their bad feelings into the pie, and without realizing it, the Wompananny witches had made one mean pizza.

HOLY ROLLING MEATBALLS!

The pizza barreled its way down the busy block.

The sisters did all they could to stop it.

Hours passed. Grown-ups were too busy panicking to make dinner, and their children were getting hungry.

One ravenous child, who never
listened when told not to eat
things off the ground, sneaked
a taste of cheese that had splattered
on her stoop.

She had to have more. The girl took off after the delicious pizza, and flocks of hungry children followed.

The pizza rumbled into the park
with the pack hot on its crust.

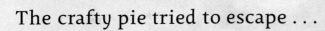
The crafty pie tried to escape . . .

. . . but it was no match for the hungry kids.

The children loved eating the pizza as much as the sisters loved making it.
And there is always a place in a witch's heart for anyone who loves her cooking.

The Wompananny Witches got right to work. They had a lot of hungry mouths to feed. Anita and Winnifred's new pizza paired flavors to please the wildest of appetites.

But the best combination of all was the one the sisters least expected.

The illustrations in this book were made with ink, watercolor, and Photoshop.

Cataloging-in-Publication Data has been applied
for and may be obtained from the Library of Congress.
ISBN: 978-1-4197-2642-2

Text and illustrations copyright © 2017 Jennie Palmer
Book design by Alyssa Nassner

Printed and bound in China
10 9 8 7 6 5 4 3 2 1

Abrams Books for Young Readers are available
at special discounts when purchased in quantity
for premiums and promotions as well as fundraising
or educational use. Special editions can also
be created to specification. For details,
contact specialsales@abramsbooks.com
or the address below.

ABRAMS The Art of Books
115 West 18th Street, New York, NY 10011
abramsbooks.com

*To Dave Palmer-Palmer
and Friday night pizza hangs*